The Old Lighthouse

David J Cooper

Published by David J Cooper, 2024.

This is a work of fiction. Similarities to real people, places, or events are entirely coincidental.

THE OLD LIGHTHOUSE

First edition. July 19, 2024.

Copyright © 2024 David J Cooper.

ISBN: 979-8227460974

Written by David J Cooper.

Table of Contents

Chapter 1..1

Chapter 2..7

Chapter 3..13

Chapter 4..19

Chapter 5..25

Chapter 6..31

Chapter 7..37

Chapter 8..43

Chapter 9..49

Chapter 10..55

Chapter 11..61

Chapter 12..67

Epilogue..73

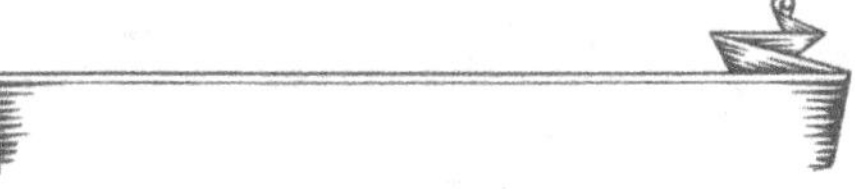

Introduction

In the remote corners of the world, where the storm-tossed seas meet the craggy cliffs, stand solitary sentinels of a bygone era — lighthouses. These beacons, once vital navigational aids for seafarers, now serve as haunting reminders of both the strength and fragility of human endeavors against nature's unrelenting power.

"The Old Lighthouse" is a journey into one such sentinel — a forsaken lighthouse perched on a rugged cliff, shrouded in mystery and whispered legends. Its weather-beaten facade and darkened lantern room tell a story of solitude and abandonment, but beneath its surface lies a tale far darker than the stormy nights it has withstood.

As the winds howl and the waves crash against the cliffs, the lighthouse remains a silent witness to secrets long buried. Its walls, steeped in history, have seen the rise and fall of countless ships and the unspoken fears of those who have manned its beacon. The isolation of the lighthouse serves as a backdrop to an unsettling narrative — a story of courage, curiosity, and the unknown forces that linger just beyond the veil of human understanding.

In this book, we follow Ella Parker, a historian drawn to the lighthouse by its enigmatic past and the whispers of its dark history. As she steps into its eerie silence, she becomes entwined with the lighthouse's tragic legacy. The storm that rages outside mirrors the tumultuous journey she is about to embark on — a journey into the heart of darkness where the past and present collide in a chilling dance.

Prepare yourself for a tale that blends historical intrigue with supernatural terror. The story that unfolds within these pages will take you through shadowy halls, across storm-swept cliffs, and into the depths of a mystery that has lain dormant for far too long. As you turn the pages, remember that the lighthouse's light, once a symbol of hope and guidance, now harbours a darkness that threatens to consume all who dare to uncover its secrets.

Welcome to "The Old Lighthouse."

Chapter 1

Ella Parker's hands gripped the steering wheel tightly as the car navigated the treacherous, winding road. Her mind was a whirlwind of anticipation and anxiety. As a historian specializing in maritime history, she had always been fascinated by shipwrecks and lighthouses. The tales surrounding this particular lighthouse had piqued her curiosity to an unsettling degree. She glanced at the old map spread across the passenger seat, tracing the route to the lighthouse with her finger. The storm outside matched her turbulent thoughts, each rumble of thunder a reminder of the challenges ahead.

The road became progressively narrower and more rugged as she ascended the cliff. The fog grew thicker, swirling around her headlights like an ominous veil. The rain lashed against the windshield with relentless force, and the car's engine sputtered. For a moment, she feared it might give out entirely. She pulled over to the side of the road, stepping out into the torrential downpour to check the engine. Her flashlight beam revealed nothing but waterlogged components and growing frustration. The storm seemed to mock her as she wrestled with the engine, each gust of wind driving her deeper into determination.

With a final, frustrated grunt, she managed to get the car started again. The engine roared to life, but the journey was far from over. She resumed driving, her hands trembling slightly as she gripped the wheel. The road twisted and turned, the fog pressing in around her like a living entity. Occasionally, she would catch a glimpse of the churning sea through the gaps in the fog, the waves crashing violently against the rocks below.

As she finally reached the base of the lighthouse, her heart sank. The structure, silhouetted against the stormy sky, was even more imposing up close. Its white paint had long since peeled away, replaced by layers of grime and rust. The lantern room at the top was dark, a gaping void against the churning sea. The wind howled mournfully, carrying with it the smell of brine and decay. Ella's flashlight beam cut through the thick fog, revealing the broken glass of the lantern room and the overgrown weeds that clawed at the base of the building.

She stepped out of the car, feeling the full brunt of the storm's fury. The cold wind whipped around her, and the salty sea spray stung her cheeks. She wrapped her coat tightly around herself and grabbed her flashlight and notebook. The path to the lighthouse was narrow and overgrown, flanked by brambles and wild grass that clawed at her legs as she walked. Each step was a battle against nature's elements, but her determination kept her moving forward.

The heavy wooden door of the lighthouse was partially ajar, creaking on its hinges. She pushed it open with a groan, the sound echoing through the empty hallway. The air inside was colder and mustier, carrying the scent of mildew and damp wood. She shivered as she crossed the threshold, her flashlight illuminating the dust-covered interior. The contrast between the howling storm outside and the eerie silence within was striking.

The main room of the lighthouse was a shadowy expanse of cobwebs and forgotten relics. The floorboards creaked underfoot as she walked through, her flashlight revealing old, weathered furniture — an ornate desk covered in dust, a chair with its upholstery tattered and faded. Nautical charts, once meticulously arranged, were now scattered haphazardly across the walls. The air was filled with a musty, stale odor, and the only sounds were the occasional drip of water and the distant rumble of thunder.

She carefully examined the various items she found. She picked up a dusty logbook from a side table, its leather cover cracked and worn. The pages were filled with handwritten entries, some barely legible due to age. A faded photograph fell out as she flipped through the book — an old, sepia-toned image of a lighthouse keeper and his family, their faces obscured by shadow. On a nearby shelf, she noticed a strange symbol etched into the wood, partially hidden under layers of grime.

As she continued her investigation, she couldn't shake the feeling that she was being watched. The temperature seemed to drop suddenly, and she noticed her breath forming visible puffs in the cold air. The wind outside grew louder, its mournful howling blending with occasional, inexplicable noises inside the lighthouse — soft whispers and the distant sound of footsteps echoing through the empty halls. Her pulse quickened, and she glanced around nervously, feeling a growing sense of dread.

The storm intensified, and the lighthouse seemed to groan in response. She moved cautiously through the building, her flashlight casting erratic shadows on the walls. She found herself drawn to the spiral staircase leading up to the lantern room. The staircase was narrow and worn, the steps creaking ominously beneath her feet. Each step seemed to echo louder than the last, creating a rhythm that mirrored the pounding of her heart.

As she ascended, she noticed the walls were lined with old, faded paintings of seascapes and shipwrecks. They were coated in dust, their colors muted by time. The wind howled through the broken windows of the lantern room, causing the remaining shards of glass to rattle against the frames. She could see the storm in full force now, the lightning illuminating the turbulent sea below. The view was both breathtaking and unnerving, a stark reminder of the lighthouse's isolation.

She set up her camera and audio equipment in the lantern room, determined to capture any paranormal activity. She arranged her sleeping area in one corner, her mind racing with the possibilities of what might lie ahead. As she settled in, the storm outside seemed to reach a crescendo, the wind shrieking and the rain battering the lighthouse's exterior with unrelenting force.

The night grew darker, and the lighthouse took on an even more foreboding presence. Ella's breath misted in the cold air, and the shadows seemed to stretch and shift in the dim light. She reviewed her notes, trying to focus on her research despite the unsettling atmosphere. The feeling of being watched grew stronger, and she glanced around the room nervously.

The sound of the wind was punctuated by occasional, unnerving noises —footsteps or creaks that didn't seem to match the storm's rhythm. She glanced towards the lantern room's darkened corners, the shadows there seeming almost to pulse with an ominous energy. Her anxiety grew with each passing hour, the eerie silence broken only by the howling storm outside and the occasional, inexplicable sound from within the lighthouse.

As she prepared for a long night of investigation, she couldn't shake the feeling that the lighthouse held more secrets than she had anticipated. The storm outside raged on, and the lighthouse, with its dark past and mysterious presence, seemed to come alive with an unsettling energy. She took a deep breath and steeled herself for the night ahead. The lighthouse promised to reveal its secrets, but at what cost?

Her thoughts raced as she glanced at the strange symbol etched into the floorboards, partially obscured by dust. It seemed to pulse with a faint, unearthly glow, hinting at the mysteries waiting to be uncovered. The night promised to be long and filled with revelations, both terrifying and profound. Her determination burned bright, even as the shadows of the lighthouse seemed to close in around her, hinting at the dangers that lay ahead.

Chapter 2

Ella Parker awoke to an unsettling silence. The storm outside had finally abated, leaving only the occasional drip of water from the leaking roof and the faint rustle of the wind. The early morning light filtered weakly through the broken panes of the lighthouse's lantern room, casting long, ghostly shadows across the floor. She stretched, her muscles aching from the uncomfortable makeshift bed. The remnants of the storm had left the lighthouse feeling colder and more desolate than ever. Her breath misted in the frigid air as she rose, determined to uncover more about the lighthouse's secrets.

Descending from the lantern room, she made her way to the main floor, where the first light of dawn revealed the true state of the lighthouse's interior. The dust-covered furniture and scattered nautical charts seemed almost to come alive in the dim light, their outlines more defined and less menacing. She took a deep breath, trying to shake off the lingering unease from the previous night. The oppressive stillness of the lighthouse was punctuated only by the occasional creak of the old building.

She focused on the desk she had found earlier. It had initially seemed like an ordinary piece of furniture, but now appeared to be a crucial part of the lighthouse's mysterious past. Carefully, she began to clear off the thick layer of dust, revealing a stack of old papers and letters. They were yellowed with age, tied together with a fraying ribbon. The handwriting was elegant but difficult to decipher.

The letters were addressed to Lydia from someone named Edmund, the lighthouse keeper. They spoke of strange occurrences and feelings of unease. Lydia's responses hinted at her own fears, describing eerie visions and an overwhelming sense of dread. "Something is not right here," one letter read, "The air is heavy with a presence I cannot name." Ella's curiosity was piqued, and she made detailed notes about the correspondence, hoping these insights would shed light on the lighthouse's dark history.

Next, she turned her attention to the old logbook she had discovered the previous night. It was filled with entries detailing daily routines and weather conditions. As she flipped through the pages, one entry stood out. The handwriting had become increasingly erratic and fragmented, describing a series of bizarre and terrifying events. The final entry was a chilling proclamation: "They are coming. The darkness will never leave."

Ella's unease deepened as she continued her investigation. She stumbled upon a hidden compartment in the wall behind a bookshelf. The compartment was small and concealed, accessible only by moving the shelf aside. Inside, she discovered a collection of old maps and journals, their pages brittle with age. One journal, in particular, caught her attention. It was bound in dark leather, with a peculiar symbol embossed on the cover.

The journal's contents were a mix of sketches, notes, and cryptic symbols. One page depicted a strange ritual involving the lighthouse, with detailed instructions and diagrams. The ritual seemed to focus on summoning and controlling an entity, and the symbols matched those she had seen etched into the walls and floors. The discovery was unsettling, hinting at the possibility that the lighthouse was a focal point for dark supernatural forces.

As the day progressed, her sense of unease grew. The lighthouse, which had seemed so quiet and still, now felt as though it was shifting and whispering around her. Shadows seemed to move just beyond the reach of her flashlight, and the temperature fluctuated unpredictably. She could not shake the feeling of being watched, her every step echoing through the empty halls with an unnatural resonance.

While exploring the lantern room again, she noticed that the air seemed thicker and more oppressive. The strange symbols she had seen the night before appeared to be more than mere decoration; they seemed to pulse with a faint, eerie glow. She recorded her observations in detail, but her notes were increasingly punctuated with her growing anxiety. The feeling of dread was almost noticeable, as if the very walls of the lighthouse were alive with a malevolent presence.

Her exploration led her to the lower levels of the lighthouse, where she discovered a hidden door concealed behind a rusted metal panel. It was partially obscured by debris, and she had to pry it open with considerable effort. The door led to a small, dimly lit room filled with old nautical equipment and more mysterious artifacts. The room smelled of dampness and decay, adding to the sense of foreboding.

In this hidden room, Ella found an old, dusty chest. Inside, she discovered various items, including a tarnished brass compass, a collection of old keys, and an ornate box with intricate carvings. The box was locked, and she spent some time trying to open it. When she finally succeeded, she discovered a collection of old, yellowed documents and a small, intricately carved figurine of a lighthouse keeper. The figurine was finely detailed, its expression inscrutable and its eyes seeming to follow her movements.

As evening approached, the lighthouse seemed to grow darker and more oppressive. The lights flickered unpredictably, and the wind outside howled with an eerie intensity. The temperature dropped suddenly, and Ella felt a cold draft moving through the rooms, as if the lighthouse itself were breathing.

The most disturbing incident occurred when she heard a distinct knock coming from the door to the hidden room. The knock was rhythmic and deliberate, a sound that did not match the random creaks and groans of the old building. She approached the door cautiously, her flashlight casting jittery shadows on the walls. When she opened it, she found nothing but an empty room and the lingering echo of the knock.

As night settled in, Ella reviewed her findings with a growing sense of urgency. The letters, journal, and artifacts all pointed towards a dark and malevolent force connected to the lighthouse. The ritual described in the journal, coupled with the strange occurrences she had experienced, suggested that the lighthouse might be a focal point for supernatural activity. The evidence was mounting, and her sense of dread was matched only by her determination to uncover the truth.

She set up her equipment once more, hoping to capture any evidence of paranormal phenomena. The night was still and quiet, save for the occasional creak of the old building. Her nerves were on edge as she waited, her flashlight casting long, jittery shadows on the walls. The silence was punctuated by the sound of the wind outside, which seemed to carry a mournful, almost plaintive quality.

As midnight approached, she saw a shadow move across the wall in the lantern room. It was fleeting, almost imperceptible, but it was enough to make her heart race. She immediately grabbed her camera and began recording, her hands shaking with a mix of fear and excitement. The shadow seemed to shift and pulse, moving in a way that was not entirely natural. Her flashlight flickered, casting erratic patterns on the walls. She could feel a presence growing stronger, and the air seemed to thicken with a supernatural energy.

Her night was marked by a series of disturbing visions. As she reviewed her recordings, she noticed faint, ghostly images appearing in the background of her footage. These images were fleeting, barely perceptible, but they seemed to depict scenes from the past — figures in old-fashioned clothing, shadowy figures moving through the lighthouse. The visions grew more intense as the night wore on, culminating in a chilling image of a figure standing at the top of the stairs. The figure was shrouded in darkness, its features obscured, but it radiated an aura of malevolence. Ella's heart pounded as she watched the footage, feeling a deep sense of dread.

As dawn approached, she was exhausted but resolute. The lighthouse had proven to be a treasure trove of secrets, but each discovery seemed to lead to more questions. The strange occurrences and unsettling experiences had left her feeling vulnerable and anxious. She took one last look around the lighthouse before retiring for the day. The hidden room, the strange artifacts, and the mysterious figure were all pieces of a puzzle she was determined to solve. As she prepared for another night of investigation, she couldn't shake the feeling that the lighthouse held more than just historical significance — it was a gateway to something far darker.

Her resolve was strengthened by her findings, but she knew that the challenges ahead would be even greater. The lighthouse, with its dark past and malevolent presence, promised to reveal its secrets in time. For now, she could only prepare herself for the unknown and hope that she would uncover the truth before it was too late.

Chapter 3

The next day dawned with a fragile calmness, a stark contrast to the previous night's relentless storm. Ella Parker stood at the base of the lighthouse, the chill of the morning air biting at her skin. She took a deep breath, steeling herself for another day of investigation. The events of the past two days had left her both intrigued and unnerved. The lighthouse was clearly more than a relic of maritime history; it was a place steeped in mystery and dark forces.

She decided to start her day by exploring the surrounding grounds. The lighthouse was perched on a desolate cliff, overlooking the churning sea. The land around it was overgrown with wild grasses and brambles, remnants of old pathways barely visible under the vegetation. As she walked, her mind raced with thoughts of the letters, the journal, and the strange artifacts she had found.

Her footsteps led her to a small, dilapidated shed near the edge of the cliff. The wooden structure looked as though it hadn't been touched in decades, its roof sagging and walls covered in moss. She pushed open the creaking door, the hinges groaning in protest. Inside, she found a collection of old tools and fishing gear, all covered in a thick layer of dust and cobwebs.

In one corner, an old rowboat lay overturned, its wood rotting and splintered.

Her eyes were drawn to a large, weathered trunk in the far corner of the shed. She approached it cautiously, her heart pounding with anticipation. The trunk was locked, but the metal clasp was rusty and brittle. With some effort, she managed to break it open. Inside, she discovered a collection of old maritime maps, a rusty sextant, and a bundle of letters tied with a faded blue ribbon.

The letters were addressed to Edmund, the lighthouse keeper, from various correspondents. They spoke of shipwrecks, strange lights seen at sea, and inexplicable disappearances. One letter, in particular, caught her eye. It was from a sailor named James, who described a harrowing encounter with a ghostly ship that appeared out of nowhere, only to vanish moments later. The sailor warned Edmund to be cautious, hinting at a dark presence that seemed to haunt the waters around the lighthouse.

Ella carefully documented the contents of the trunk, adding them to her growing collection of evidence. As she worked, she couldn't shake the feeling of being watched. The hairs on the back of her neck stood on end, and she turned abruptly, scanning the shadows of the shed. There was nothing there, but the sense of unease lingered.

Returning to the lighthouse, she decided to delve deeper into the hidden room she had discovered the day before. The room had yielded several intriguing artifacts, but she had the feeling there was more to uncover. She descended the spiral staircase to the lower levels, the air growing colder and damper with each step.

The hidden room was as she had left it, filled with nautical equipment and mysterious relics. Her eyes were drawn to the old, dusty chest she had opened previously. Something about the chest felt incomplete, as if it held more secrets yet to be discovered. She examined it more closely, running her fingers along the intricate carvings on its surface. To her surprise, she found a hidden compartment at the base of the chest.

With a sense of triumph, she opened the compartment. Inside, she found a small, leather-bound book and a strange, metallic object. The book was a diary, filled with handwritten entries that seemed to date back over a century. The object was a peculiar amulet, adorned with symbols that matched those she had seen etched into the walls and floors of the lighthouse.

She sat down and began to read the diary. It belonged to Lydia, the wife of Edmund, the lighthouse keeper. The entries detailed her descent into madness, driven by the malevolent presence that seemed to haunt the lighthouse. Lydia described seeing ghostly apparitions, hearing disembodied voices, and experiencing vivid nightmares. She believed that the lighthouse was cursed, and that the amulet she had found was a key to controlling the dark forces within.

The final entry was particularly chilling. Lydia wrote of a ritual she had performed in a desperate attempt to banish the evil presence. She believed that the amulet held the power to either trap or release the entity, depending on the intentions of the one who wielded it. Lydia's last words were a warning: "Beware the darkness. It seeks to consume all who dare to uncover its secrets."

Ella felt a shiver run down her spine. The pieces of the puzzle were beginning to come together, but the picture they formed was far from comforting. The lighthouse was a focal point for supernatural activity, and the amulet was somehow tied to its power. Ella knew she had to be cautious, but her determination to uncover the truth was stronger than ever.

As night fell, she prepared for another vigil in the lantern room. She set up her equipment, including cameras, audio recorders, and motion sensors. The amulet rested on the desk in front of her, its metallic surface reflecting the dim light. Her mind raced with possibilities, her thoughts filled with Lydia's warnings and the strange occurrences she had witnessed.

The lighthouse was eerily quiet, the only sounds being the occasional creak of the old building and the distant crash of waves against the cliffs. She sat in silence, her eyes fixed on the amulet. She couldn't shake the feeling that it was watching her, its symbols pulsing with a faint, otherworldly glow.

As midnight approached, the temperature in the lantern room dropped suddenly. She could see her breath misting in the cold air, and the shadows seemed to grow deeper and more menacing. The wind outside picked up, howling through the broken windows and rattling the remaining shards of glass.

Her heart raced as she saw a shadow move across the wall. It was faint at first, barely perceptible, but it grew more defined with each passing moment. The shadow took on the shape of a figure, tall and gaunt, its features obscured. She grabbed her camera and began recording, her hands trembling with a mix of fear and excitement.

The figure seemed to move closer, its shadowy form becoming more distinct. Ella could feel a visible sense of malevolence emanating from it, a cold, suffocating presence that filled the room. She held her breath, her eyes locked on the figure as it approached the amulet.

Suddenly, the amulet began to glow with an intense, white light. The figure recoiled, its shadowy form distorting and flickering. Ella watched in awe and terror as the light from the amulet grew brighter, pushing the figure back. The room was filled with a deafening roar, and the air seemed to crackle with energy.

With a final, agonized scream, the figure vanished, leaving behind an eerie silence. The light from the amulet faded, and the room was plunged back into darkness. Ella sat in stunned silence, her heart pounding in her chest. She had witnessed something extraordinary, something beyond her wildest imagination.

As the first light of dawn began to filter through the broken windows, she knew that her journey was far from over. The lighthouse held many more secrets, and the amulet was the key to uncovering them. She took a deep breath, her resolve stronger than ever. The darkness had been pushed back, but the battle was far from won. Ella was determined to uncover the truth, no matter the cost.

Chapter 4

Ella awoke to the stillness of the lighthouse, the early morning light filtering weakly through the fractured panes of the lantern room. The storm had finally passed, leaving behind a damp, eerie calm. As she stretched, her muscles ached from the previous night's uncomfortable rest. The remnants of the storm had made the lighthouse colder and more desolate than before. Her breath misted in the frigid air, and the faint rustle of the wind through the broken windows added to the sense of unease.

Determined to uncover more of the lighthouse's secrets, Ella prepared for a thorough exploration of the surrounding grounds. The cryptic journal entries and peculiar occurrences the night before suggested that there might be more to discover outside the lighthouse. The fog that still lingered around the cliffs wrapped the landscape in an almost tangible silence, heightening the sense of isolation.

Navigating the soggy, uneven terrain proved challenging. Her boots sank into the muddy earth with each step, and the remnants of the storm had made the path slippery and treacherous. She carefully made her way to the edge of the cliff, where she had noticed the unusual rock formation during her previous exploration. The rocks formed a rough circle, their arrangement appearing deliberate and oddly structured.

Clearing away the debris and tangled vines, Ella revealed what seemed to be the remnants of an old fire pit.

The stones were blackened and scorched, suggesting frequent use. The symbols etched into the stones matched those she had seen in Lydia's diary and the journal. The fire pit was clearly not just a simple structure; it had been used for rituals or ceremonies. She took photographs and made sketches of the symbols, noting their similarity to the ritualistic patterns found in the hidden room.

Returning to the lighthouse, her sense of anticipation grew. The building seemed to hum with a latent energy, and the silence was punctuated only by the distant drip of water and the occasional groan of the old structure. She focused on revisiting the hidden room and its contents. The peculiar aura of the lighthouse seemed to thicken as she approached, heightening her awareness of every creak and shift in the building.

She spread out the documents she had found: the letters, the journal, and the map. The map revealed additional markings, including several hidden locations that had not been noted before. The annotations on the map hinted at points of interest that could be linked to the lighthouse's dark history. The idea of undiscovered locations added to her mounting excitement and apprehension.

Her focus was soon interrupted by an unsettling noise — a rhythmic, deliberate tapping coming from the upper levels. Her heart raced. The sound was unlike the usual creaks and groans of the old building. Driven by curiosity and a growing sense of dread, she decided to investigate.

Ascending the spiral staircase, she felt an unmistakable drop in temperature with each step. The lantern room, once a place of relative safety, now felt charged with an almost unmistakeable tension. The tapping grew louder, its rhythmic nature creating an eerie contrast to the surrounding silence. Her flashlight cast jittery patterns on the walls, making shadows dance and flicker.

As she reached the top of the stairs, the tapping abruptly ceased. Her pulse quickened as she searched the lantern room. The floorboards there seemed to have been disturbed recently. She noticed that the wood was discolored, forming a pattern that matched some of the symbols from the amulet and Lydia's journal. It was as though the lighthouse itself was trying to communicate with her.

With a mixture of trepidation and determination, she used a crowbar to pry up the discolored floorboards. Beneath them, she uncovered a small iron box, rusted and ancient. She recalled the collection of old keys she had discovered earlier and, after some trial and error, found one that fit the lock.

The box creaked open to reveal a stack of aged letters and a faded map. The map depicted the lighthouse and its surroundings, but with additional markings and annotations indicating hidden locations. The letters, written in a frantic scrawl, were correspondence between Edmund and an unidentified party. They described an escalation of supernatural occurrences and a plan to perform a ritual to "contain the darkness" and prevent it from escaping the lighthouse.

One letter detailed a specific date for the ritual, which coincided with the anniversary of a notorious shipwreck that had occurred near the lighthouse. This connection suggested a deep-seated link between the shipwreck and the lighthouse's dark history. The urgency in Edmund's letters revealed his desperation to control the malevolent force that seemed to be growing stronger.

As dusk approached, the lighthouse took on an even more oppressive and sinister atmosphere. The wind outside howled with an unsettling intensity, and the temperature dropped sharply. Ella prepared for another night of investigation, setting up additional equipment in hopes of capturing evidence of paranormal activity.

The night deepened, and the lighthouse grew darker and more oppressive. The wind outside seemed to carry a mournful, almost plaintive quality. Ella's nerves were stretched thin as she reviewed her findings and equipment. The shadows in the lantern room seemed to lengthen and twist in the dim light, and the silence was occasionally broken by the haunting sounds of the wind and the distant creaks of the old building.

As midnight approached, she noticed a peculiar phenomenon. Shadows on the walls appeared to shift and pulse with an unnatural rhythm, and the air grew thicker with a substantial energy. Her flashlight flickered intermittently, casting erratic patterns. The sense of a presence — something malevolent and powerful — grew stronger.

Ella reviewed her recordings, noticing faint, ghostly images appearing in the footage. These images were fleeting but seemed to depict scenes from the past — figures in old-fashioned clothing and shadowy forms moving through the lighthouse. The visions intensified as the night wore on, culminating in a chilling image of a dark figure standing at the top of the stairs. Its features were obscured, but it radiated an aura of malevolence that sent a shiver down Ella's spine.

Exhausted but resolute, she took one last look around the lighthouse before retiring for the night. The hidden room, the strange artifacts, and the mysterious figure were all pieces of a puzzle she was determined to solve. The lighthouse, with its dark past and malevolent presence, promised to reveal its secrets in time. For now, Ella could only prepare herself for whatever lay ahead and hope that she would uncover the truth before it was too late.

As the shadows grew longer and the wind howled outside, she braced herself for the challenges yet to come. The lighthouse held its secrets close, but Ella was determined to uncover them, no matter the cost. The coming days would test her courage and resolve, and she knew that the path to truth would be fraught with danger and discovery.

Chapter 5

Ella Parker woke to an eerie calm, the remnants of the storm leaving an unsettling stillness in the air. The morning sun, struggling through the broken panes of the lantern room, cast weak, ghostly shadows across the cold floor. The lighthouse, having weathered the tempest, stood in an oppressive silence, as if holding its breath. Her breath misted in the cold air as she rose, feeling both the weight of her discoveries and a renewed sense of purpose. The previous night's unsettling findings — the cryptic journal, the ominous symbols, and the shadowy figure — had only deepened the enigma surrounding the lighthouse.

She began her day by revisiting the journal and the map she had discovered. The map, marked with cryptic annotations and symbols, had hinted at several significant locations. One of these was marked with a troubling note: "The Heart of the Darkness." Ella's instincts told her that this location might hold the key to unlocking the lighthouse's secrets.

After a quick breakfast, she prepared her gear for exploration: rope, a climbing harness, and a rugged flashlight. The weather had cleared, but the cliffside remained treacherous. The previous storm had left the terrain slick and unstable. Ella knew she would need to be cautious as she made her way towards the designated spot.

The climb was gruelling. The path was narrow, flanked by jagged rocks and overgrown vegetation. Every step was a battle against the elements, with the wind howling relentlessly and the ground shifting beneath her feet. Ella's heart pounded as she navigated the precarious trail. When she finally reached the edge of the cliff, she was greeted by a scene that was both awe-inspiring and unsettling.

There, partially obscured by debris and encroaching vegetation, stood a weathered stone structure. It resembled an ancient altar, its surface etched with the same enigmatic symbols she had encountered in the lighthouse. The structure was partially buried under layers of moss and lichen, and the symbols carved into it were worn but still visible. The altar seemed to pulsate with an almost imperceptible energy, and Ella could not shake the feeling that it was watching her.

Her hands shook slightly as she pried open a loose stone on the altar. Inside, she found a small compartment containing a rusted key and a piece of parchment. The parchment, though brittle with age, was legible. Its ink had faded, but the words were clear enough: "The heart must be awakened. The circle will bind." The message was cryptic but suggested a connection between the altar and the lighthouse's deeper mysteries.

With this new lead, Ella made her way back to the lighthouse, her mind racing with possibilities. The connection between the altar, the key, and the cryptic message pointed to a larger, more intricate narrative. She decided to investigate another location indicated on the map: a dilapidated boathouse near the base of the cliffs.

The boathouse, battered by time and weather, was in a state of ruin. Its wooden walls were warped and rotting, and the door hung loosely on its hinges. Ella pushed it open with some effort, and the scent of mildew and decay hit her immediately. Inside, the air was thick with the musty smell of old wood and stagnant water. The light from her flashlight cut through the gloom, revealing a cluttered interior filled with broken nautical equipment and scattered debris.

In a dark corner of the boathouse, partially obscured by fallen timbers, she spotted a small, locked chest. The chest was encrusted with rust, and its surface was covered in grime. Using the key she had discovered at the altar, she unlocked the chest with a satisfying click. Inside, she found a collection of old nautical charts, their edges frayed and yellowed with age. Among the charts was a dark leather-bound journal marked with the same symbol found in the lighthouse's journal.

Ella's fingers trembled with anticipation as she opened the journal. The pages were filled with detailed notes and sketches of various shipwrecks. The journal's entries described not just the physical details of the wrecks but also a series of eerie phenomena and supernatural occurrences. One entry in particular caught her eye. It detailed the disappearance of a ship named "The Tempest," which had vanished mysteriously. The ship's crew had reported strange occurrences and an overwhelming sense of dread before their disappearance. The journal suggested that the lighthouse might be connected to the ship's fate.

Ella also discovered several letters and documents in the chest. These discussed the lighthouse's dark reputation and the need for rituals to protect the surrounding area. The documents included diagrams of the symbols she had seen in the lighthouse and instructions for performing protective rituals. They hinted that the lighthouse was central to attempts to contain or banish a malevolent force.

As evening approached, her sense of urgency grew. The boathouse had provided valuable information but had also deepened the mystery. The connection between the lighthouse, the altar, and the boathouse suggested that the lighthouse was not merely a historical site but a focal point for dark forces.

Back at the lighthouse, Ella set up her equipment, preparing for another night of investigation. The wind outside had picked up, its howling taking on an eerie, almost mournful quality that seemed to seep into the building. The temperature inside the lighthouse had dropped noticeably, and the shadows in the lantern room appeared to stretch and shift with an unnatural energy.

Ella reviewed her footage from the previous night. The shadowy figures she had captured seemed to follow a specific pattern, mirroring the ritualistic movements described in the journal. The figure she had seen earlier appeared to perform a series of motions that matched the diagrams in the journal, reinforcing the idea that the lighthouse was a site of ongoing supernatural activity.

As night fell, the atmosphere in the lighthouse grew increasingly oppressive. The temperature continued to drop, and the shadows seemed to pulse with a life of their own. Ella's flashlight flickered unpredictably, casting erratic patterns on the walls. The building groaned and creaked, its old bones seemingly reacting to the growing energy.

At midnight, she noticed a shadow moving across the wall in the lantern room. It was fleeting but distinct, and her heart raced as she grabbed her camera. The shadow seemed to shift and pulse, moving in a way that defied natural explanation. The air around her felt heavy, charged with an unearthly presence. Ella's flashlight flickered and dimmed, and the temperature in the room seemed to drop even further.

As she reviewed the footage, she saw faint, ghostly images in the background. These images depicted scenes from the past — figures in old-fashioned clothing and shadowy forms moving through the lighthouse. The visions intensified as the night wore on, culminating in a chilling image of a dark figure standing at the top of the stairs. The figure's features were obscured, but its presence radiated a palpable sense of malevolence.

Ella's nerves were on edge as dawn approached. The lighthouse had revealed many secrets, but each discovery seemed to lead to more questions. The strange occurrences, the artifacts, and the supernatural activity all pointed to a deeper mystery. As she prepared for another night of investigation, Ella knew that the coming hours would be crucial in uncovering the truth about the lighthouse's dark past. The answers she sought were just beyond her grasp, and she braced herself for whatever lay ahead.

Chapter 6

Dawn broke with a grey, overcast light that did little to dispel the lingering gloom within the lighthouse. The storm had passed, but its effects were still felt. The lighthouse stood silent and brooding, its exterior battered by the tempest's fury. Inside, Ella Parker's mood mirrored the desolate weather as she continued her investigation into the lighthouse's dark secrets.

She started her day by reviewing the previous night's findings. The spectral figure she had seen in her footage and the chilling inscriptions she had deciphered from the hidden chamber weighed heavily on her mind. She spread out the various documents she had found — the old nautical charts, letters, and the leather-bound book — on a dusty table in the main room. Each piece of evidence seemed to form a fragment of a larger, sinister puzzle.

She meticulously examined the nautical charts, noting the unusual symbols and markings that appeared in various places. Many of these symbols matched those she had seen etched into the walls and floors of the lighthouse. It seemed clear that these symbols were not random but part of a larger system of rites or rituals designed to either control or contain something dark and powerful.

Her attention then shifted to the letters she had discovered. They were written by individuals who had lived and worked at the lighthouse long before its abandonment. The letters detailed escalating fears and strange occurrences, including inexplicable phenomena such as flickering lights, sudden drops in temperature, and shadowy figures moving through the lighthouse. The growing sense of dread expressed in the letters suggested that the lighthouse was a place where fear and darkness had taken root.

The worn leather-bound book, which appeared to be a detailed historical account, provided more context. It described the lighthouse's construction and early use, but also mentioned an "ancient malevolence" that seemed to have been present from the very beginning. The book detailed various rituals performed by the lighthouse keepers to combat or appease this malevolence, hinting at a dark purpose behind the lighthouse's creation.

Ella was interrupted by a sudden, loud crash from the upper levels. Her heart raced as she grabbed her flashlight and ascended the narrow, creaking staircase. Each step seemed to reverberate with a sense of foreboding. She reached the lantern room, finding it in disarray. Papers and charts were scattered, and the old desk had been overturned. The chaotic scene suggested a deliberate disturbance rather than a simple accident.

Among the debris, her flashlight beam illuminated a small, intricately carved box partially hidden beneath the overturned desk. The box was covered in symbols that matched those she had seen before. With trembling hands, she used the key she had found earlier to unlock the box. The creaking lid revealed its contents: a collection of old letters and a worn, leather-bound book.

The letters were addressed to various individuals, each describing increasingly disturbing events. They spoke of disappearances, sightings of shadowy figures, and a pervasive sense of dread. One letter, dated several years before the lighthouse's abandonment, detailed the writer's growing fear of a "presence that cannot be named," suggesting that the malevolence described in the historical book was real and active.

The leather-bound book was a detailed account of the lighthouse's history, written by an unknown author. It described not only the lighthouse's construction but also the rituals performed by the keepers to ward off the ancient evil. The book mentioned a hidden chamber beneath the lighthouse, accessible only through a secret passage, and hinted at the importance of this chamber in the ritualistic practices.

Ella's determination to uncover the truth was renewed by these findings. She examined the lantern room more closely, noting faint markings on the floor that seemed to form part of a larger design. Her flashlight revealed a hidden trapdoor, its outline barely visible beneath the dust. She pried it open with effort, revealing a narrow staircase leading into darkness.

The descent into the hidden chamber was slow and treacherous. The air grew colder with each step, and the musty smell of dampness intensified. Ella's flashlight flickered erratically, casting unsettling shadows on the walls as she descended. The symbols she had seen throughout the lighthouse were more pronounced here, etched into the stone walls with meticulous care.

At the bottom of the staircase, she emerged into a dimly lit chamber. The room was cluttered with ancient relics, dusty furniture, and cobweb-covered artifacts. In the center stood a large stone altar adorned with the same symbols she had encountered elsewhere. Surrounding the altar were faded candles, their wax melted and hardened into grotesque shapes.

The chamber was suffused with a heavy, oppressive energy. She felt an intense chill as she approached the altar, where an inscription was carved into the stone: "To bind the darkness, one must become the darkness." The inscription was accompanied by cryptic symbols and diagrams, suggesting a complex ritual or binding process. The air around the altar seemed to pulse with a dark, latent power, heightening Ella's sense of foreboding.

She took out her notebook and began transcribing the inscription, her hands shaking with a mix of fear and excitement. The chamber's atmosphere was thick with an ancient, perceptible energy, and the air seemed to grow colder as she worked. The whispers she had heard earlier grew louder, their mournful tones blending into a coherent voice that spoke of despair and a timeless struggle against an ancient evil.

The voice seemed to emanate from the altar itself, its source elusive yet omnipresent. Ella's flashlight revealed old tomes scattered around the chamber, their pages yellowed and brittle. These tomes detailed various aspects of the lighthouse's history and the rituals performed within its walls. They hinted at a desperate struggle to contain or banish the entity, but the specifics remained frustratingly vague.

As evening approached, the oppressive atmosphere of the chamber seemed to grow thicker. Ella's sense of urgency increased as she realized that she was on the brink of uncovering a crucial piece of the lighthouse's dark history. The chamber's cold, heavy air and the whispering voice made it clear that the answers she sought were close but shrouded in darkness.

Back in the lantern room, she reviewed her findings with a growing sense of anticipation. The hidden chamber, the inscriptions, and the whispered voice all pointed toward a complex and disturbing ritual designed to control or banish the entity. The lighthouse was revealed not only as a historical site but as a focal point of supernatural forces.

As night fell, the lighthouse seemed to grow darker and more foreboding. The temperature dropped further, and the shadows in the lantern room appeared to pulse with an almost sentient energy. Ella braced herself for another night of investigation, knowing that the entity and the lighthouse's dark secrets were drawing her ever closer to a terrifying revelation.

Chapter 7

As the night drew to a close, Ella's exhaustion was noticeable. Her investigation had revealed unsettling truths, but the oppressive atmosphere of the lighthouse seemed to grow more formidable with each passing hour. Despite her fatigue, the cold, suffocating presence of the entity seemed to push her to her limits, forcing her to confront the dark forces that had been lying dormant for so long.

With the dawn breaking, she was greeted by the weak, greyish light filtering through the broken panes of the lantern room. The storm had passed, leaving behind a serene but deceptive calm. The remnants of the night's violence had drained the lighthouse of its tempestuous energy, leaving a deceptive tranquility in its wake. However, Ella knew that beneath this calm surface lay an ever-present danger.

She descended from the lantern room, her steps heavy with weariness. The lighthouse, bathed in the subdued morning light, seemed less menacing but no less eerie. The dust-covered furniture and scattered charts appeared less threatening in the daylight, yet the shadows still lurked with a malevolent presence. The morning light did little to dispel the sense of dread that clung to her, a lingering reminder of the entity's influence.

Determined to make sense of the unsettling discoveries from the previous night, Ella returned to the hidden chamber. The symbols on the altar, which had once seemed so disconcerting, now pulsed with a stronger, more disturbing glow. The air was thick with a distinct malice, as if the entity was aware of her intrusion and was responding with increased aggression.

The tomes she had studied earlier offered fragmented insights into the entity's nature. They described it as an ancient being that existed on a borderline, straddling the boundary between the physical world and a darker, more enigmatic realm. The entity was said to be amorphous, able to shift its form and influence its surroundings in ways that defied logical explanation. Its power grew stronger in darkness and fear, feeding off the emotional energy of those who ventured into its domain.

One particularly chilling passage detailed the entity's ability to manipulate its environment, creating illusions and feeding on the psychological vulnerabilities of its victims. The descriptions spoke of a creature that thrived on isolation and despair, using its influence to drive individuals to the brink of madness. The more fear and negativity it could generate, the stronger it became, making it a formidable and nearly unstoppable force.

Ella found a passage in one of the old books that described a ritual intended to contain the entity within a specific area. The ritual involved ancient symbols and incantations designed to create a barrier that would confine the entity's power. However, the text also warned of the ritual's limitations: if the containment was weakened or if the entity's influence grew too strong, the barrier would fail, allowing the entity to break free and extend its reach beyond the lighthouse.

The realization that the lighthouse was not just a focal point for the entity but potentially a gateway to a much larger and more dangerous realm was unsettling. The failed rituals and growing power of the entity suggested that the lighthouse had become a nexus for dark supernatural forces. The new symbols on the altar and the disturbing changes in the hidden chamber indicated that the entity was testing the boundaries of its confinement, preparing for a more significant and potentially catastrophic move.

Ella's search for the hidden chamber continued with renewed determination. She meticulously examined every corner of the lighthouse, searching for any signs of concealed passages or hidden rooms. Her efforts were rewarded when she discovered a series of old, rusted doors that had been obscured by debris. One of the doors, covered in symbols that matched those she had seen in the hidden chamber, drew her attention.

With considerable effort, she pried open the door, revealing a narrow, dimly lit passage. The air was musty and thick with the smell of decay. The passage led to a small, hidden room filled with faded paintings and ancient symbols. The walls were adorned with intricate carvings that seemed to shift and change in the dim light, creating a disorienting and unsettling effect.

At the centre of the room stood a large, ornate chest. Its surface was covered in elaborate carvings and symbols, the runes and patterns forming a complex and disturbing design. Ella approached the chest with a mixture of trepidation and hope. She knew that what lay inside could be crucial to understanding and potentially countering the entity's power.

The chest's lock was old and rusted, but she managed to open it after several tense moments. Inside, she found a collection of old documents and artifacts. Among them was a large, leather-bound book embossed with the same symbol that had appeared in the hidden chamber. The book's cover was worn but still intact, and the symbol seemed to pulsate with an almost imperceptible energy.

She carefully opened the book, revealing detailed accounts of rituals and ceremonies designed to summon and control the entity. The text was filled with complex instructions and diagrams, outlining the steps required to perform a powerful ritual that could potentially banish the entity from the lighthouse. The ritual required specific components, including ancient symbols, incantations, and a significant amount of emotional energy. The book also mentioned a rare artifact that was said to be the key to breaking the entity's hold on the lighthouse.

The discovery of the book was both a blessing and a challenge. While it provided a potential means to banish the entity, it also required Ella to obtain the rare artifact and perform the ritual under highly specific conditions. The entity's influence was growing stronger, and she knew that time was running out. She needed to act quickly to locate the artifact and prepare for the ritual.

As she reviewed the book's instructions, she felt a renewed sense of urgency. The lighthouse was no longer just a place of historical interest — it had become a battleground between light and darkness. The stakes were higher than she had ever imagined, and the entity's malevolent presence demanded immediate action.

The rare artifact mentioned in the book was said to be hidden within the lighthouse, possibly in one of the many concealed chambers or secret compartments. Ella's search for the artifact took on a new level of intensity as she meticulously combed through the lighthouse's remaining areas, examining every possible hiding spot.

Her investigation led her to a hidden compartment behind a wall panel in the lower levels of the lighthouse. The compartment was filled with old nautical equipment and artifacts, including a tarnished brass compass and a collection of old keys. Among these items was a small, intricately carved figurine of a lighthouse keeper, its expression inscrutable and its eyes seeming to follow her every move.

The figurine, while intriguing, was not the artifact she was seeking. Ella continued her search, her determination unwavering despite the mounting exhaustion and the growing sense of dread. She knew that finding the artifact was crucial to completing the ritual and breaking the entity's hold on the lighthouse.

As evening approached, the lighthouse seemed to grow darker and more oppressive. The wind outside howled with an eerie intensity, and the temperature dropped suddenly, adding to the sense of foreboding. The lights flickered unpredictably, casting long, jittery shadows on the walls.

Ella's investigation was interrupted by a series of unsettling occurrences. The shadows in the lighthouse seemed to move with a life of their own, reacting to her presence with an almost conscious awareness. The whispers that had been a faint background noise the previous night now grew louder and more insistent, their mournful tones carrying a chilling resonance.

The most disturbing incident occurred when Ella heard a rhythmic knock coming from one of the walls. The knock was deliberate and unmistakable, a sound that did not match the random creaks and groans of the old building. She approached the source of the sound cautiously, her flashlight casting jittery shadows on the walls. When she opened the wall panel, she found nothing but an empty room and the lingering echo of the knock.

Despite the growing sense of dread, Ella pressed on with her search. The lighthouse had become a maze of darkness and shadows, each corner revealing new and unsettling aspects of the entity's influence. She knew that the entity was growing stronger, testing the boundaries of its confinement, and she had to act quickly to prevent it from breaking free.

As the night approached, she reviewed her findings with a sense of mounting urgency. The tomes, symbols, and artifacts all pointed to a dark and malevolent force connected to the lighthouse. The rare artifact she sought was the key to performing the ritual and banishing the entity. The lighthouse was a battleground between light and darkness, and Ella was determined to uncover the truth and find a way to counteract the entity's growing influence.

Her resolve was unwavering. The lighthouse, with its dark past and haunting presence, held many secrets that she was determined to uncover. The entity's next move was uncertain, but Ella knew that she had to confront whatever lay ahead. The lighthouse promised to reveal its secrets in time, and Ella was prepared to face the challenges that awaited her in the darkness.

Chapter 8

Dawn's light revealed a lighthouse gripped by an unnatural stillness. The storm had passed, leaving a delicate silence in its wake, yet the air was thick with foreboding. Ella woke with a start, feeling the weight of exhaustion in her bones. Each creak of the lighthouse seemed to echo through her mind, a haunting reminder of the perilous journey she was on. Her dreams had been restless, filled with dark shapes and whispering voices, and now, as the first light of day filtered through the broken panes of the lantern room, she felt the oppressive atmosphere of the lighthouse more acutely.

Determined not to let fatigue overwhelm her, she resolved to delve deeper into the lower levels of the lighthouse. The chill in the air and the dank smell of the stone reminded her of the gravity of her mission. She gathered her equipment and descended the creaking staircase to the lighthouse's lower levels. Her footsteps echoed in the dim corridors, adding to the eerie silence that seemed to cling to every surface.

Ella began her exploration with a renewed sense of urgency. The hidden chamber she had found previously seemed to hold significant clues, and she needed to piece together the puzzle that was the lighthouse's dark history. Her flashlight illuminated dusty shelves lined with jars, vials, and strange artifacts, each one a relic of a time long forgotten. As she examined the items, she felt a shiver run down her spine — something about these artifacts seemed to resonate with an unsettling energy.

Among the artifacts, she found an old, leather-bound journal that matched the one she had discovered earlier. This journal was more worn and its cover bore the same intricate symbol. With growing apprehension, she opened the journal and began to read. The entries were written in a frantic scrawl, each one a testament to the author's increasing desperation. The writings spoke of a growing darkness, an insidious force that defied explanation and resisted all attempts to understand or control it. The author's fear was noticeable, their attempts to perform rituals described in the journal only seeming to worsen the situation.

One particular entry stood out. It described a hidden chamber beneath the lighthouse, accessible through a series of elaborate traps and illusions designed to deter any would-be intruders. The entry mentioned that this chamber was believed to hold the artifact — a small, ornately carved figurine that was central to the lighthouse's dark lore. The journal also hinted at the subterranean network that had been sealed off long ago, making it a challenging task to locate.

Ella's heart raced as she processed this information. If the hidden chamber was indeed where the artifact lay, it could be the breakthrough she needed. She resolved to find a way to access this underground network and navigate the traps described in the journal.

Returning to the main floor, she resumed her search for hidden passages or access points to the underground network. Her flashlight beam danced across the walls, revealing symbols and carvings that seemed to shift and writhe in the dim light. Each symbol appeared to be a blend of nautical motifs and arcane designs. She took detailed notes, hoping these symbols would provide clues to the artifact's location.

During her search, she was interrupted by unsettling noises. The lighthouse seemed to come alive with an eerie energy. Disembodied whispers, faint and haunting, seemed to emanate from the walls. At first, she attributed these to the building's age and the wind, but the whispers grew louder and more distinct, almost as if they were calling her name. The voices were unintelligible but carried an urgency that made her skin crawl.

Following the whispers, she discovered a hidden panel she had previously overlooked. The panel was concealed behind a stack of debris, and she had to pry it open with considerable effort. Inside was a narrow, dark passageway, and a cold draft rushed out as she opened it. She took a deep breath and ventured inside, her flashlight casting eerie shadows on the walls.

The passage led to a subterranean chamber dimly lit by flickering torches. The chamber was adorned with ancient symbols and carvings, their meanings obscured by centuries of dust. At the center stood an ornate altar covered in intricate designs. Ella's heart skipped a beat when she noticed the familiar symbol embossed on the altar — it matched the one found in the journal and on the artifact.

As she approached the altar, the atmosphere grew heavier, and the darkness seemed to close in around her. The entity's influence was recognisable, its presence growing more intense. The whispers in the chamber grew louder, almost drowning out her thoughts. They seemed to carry a mixture of ancient incantations and dire warnings.

She carefully examined the altar, searching for any clues that could lead her to the artifact. The symbols and markings on the altar were intricate and confusing. She meticulously recorded her observations, hoping they would provide insights into the artifact's location.

As she worked, the chamber was filled with an ominous creaking sound. The torches flickered erratically, casting dancing shadows on the walls. A cold draft swept through the room, making the shadows appear to writhe and twist. The entity's presence was now undeniable, its dark influence suffusing the chamber.

Ella's flashlight beam revealed a hidden compartment beneath the altar. With trembling hands, she pried it open, revealing a small, ornate box. The box was covered in intricate carvings and symbols that pulsed with a faint, eerie glow. She opened the box, her heart pounding with a mix of anticipation and dread.

Inside the box lay the artifact — a small, intricately carved figurine of a lighthouse keeper. The figurine was finely detailed, its expression inscrutable and its eyes seeming to follow her every move. It was the same as the one she had found earlier in the hidden chamber, but this one seemed to radiate a strange energy.

Her discovery was both a triumph and a challenge. The artifact was crucial for performing the ritual, but the entity's growing influence made the task even more daunting. The whispers in the chamber were growing louder, and the darkness seemed to be closing in around her.

With the artifact in hand and the ritual instructions carefully noted, Ella knew that she had to act quickly. The entity's power was growing stronger, and she needed to complete the ritual to banish it before it could extend its influence beyond the lighthouse. The lighthouse was becoming a battleground between light and darkness, and Ella was determined to confront the malevolent force and uncover the truth.

As she prepared to leave the underground chamber, she felt a growing sense of urgency. The shadows in the chamber seemed to shift and darken, and the whispers grew more insistent. The entity's presence was undeniable, and the stakes were higher than ever. Ella knew that she had to perform the ritual before it was too late, or risk unleashing the entity's malevolent power on the world.

With renewed determination, she made her way back to the main floor. The lighthouse seemed to react to her presence, its shadows growing darker and more oppressive. The whispers that had been faint background noise earlier were now a constant, insistent presence. Ella prepared for the final confrontation, ready to confront the darkness that had haunted the lighthouse for so long.

Chapter 9

The lighthouse's oppressive silence was interrupted only by the soft rustle of Ella Parker's footsteps and the occasional creak of the ancient structure. As she ascended the narrow, winding staircase back to the lantern room, her thoughts churned with the weight of her preparations. The air was thick with tension, each step she took echoing her apprehension. The lantern room, once a daunting void of shadows and fear, was now her stage for the most critical phase of her investigation: the ritual to banish the entity that had plagued the lighthouse for so long.

Ella's preparations were meticulous and methodical. The ritual required not just precision, but a deep understanding of the ancient symbols and incantations described in the journal she had found. The symbols, which had seemed enigmatic and threatening when she first discovered them, now took on a new significance. They were not just markings on the floor, but keys to a complex ritual that spanned centuries.

The lantern room was dimly lit, the soft glow from her lantern casting eerie shadows that danced along the walls. She set up her equipment with an air of quiet determination. She placed the artifact — the intricately carved figurine of the lighthouse keeper — at the centre of a carefully arranged pattern of symbols she had traced on the floor. The symbols were drawn with chalk and powdered herbs, their lines and curves forming an intricate web that seemed to pulse with a supernatural energy.

As she completed the pattern, the atmosphere in the room began to shift. The air grew heavier, and a faint, almost imperceptible hum filled the space. The symbols, once faint and inconspicuous, now seemed to radiate a dim, ethereal light. The temperature in the lantern room dropped noticeably, causing Ella's breath to mist in the chilly air. Shadows on the walls seemed to stretch and writhe, reacting to the energy that was beginning to coalesce around her.

She took a deep breath and began to recite the incantations from the journal. The words were ancient and their pronunciation was delicate and precise. As she spoke, the room seemed to come alive with the power of the ritual. The lantern flickered violently, casting erratic shadows that seemed to dance with the rhythm of her incantations. The whispers, which had been a distant murmur, now became a chorus of fragmented voices. They rose and fell in a haunting melody, their tones carrying an unsettling mix of anger and sorrow.

The entity's presence was unmistakable. Ella could feel its malevolent gaze, a cold, oppressive force that seemed to press in on her from all directions. The whispers grew louder, their voices overlapping in a dissonant symphony that filled the room. Ella focused intently on the ritual, her mind resolutely following the instructions. The figurine of the lighthouse keeper, now placed at the center of the symbol pattern, appeared to come alive with a faint, pulsating glow. Its expression, though carved with meticulous detail, seemed to shift and change, as if the figurine were reacting to the ritual's power.

With each step of the ritual, the energy in the lantern room grew more intense. Ella moved the figurine in specific patterns, as instructed by the journal, channeling the ritual's energy through the intricate network of symbols. The room was filled with a growing, almost tangible force. The air crackled with static electricity, and the shadows on the walls seemed to stretch and contort in unnatural ways. The whispers, once mere background noise, were now a cacophony of voices, their tones rising and falling in a chaotic rhythm.

The ritual reached its apex with the final incantation, a powerful invocation intended to banish the entity and seal its influence. Ella recited the words with fervor, her voice echoing through the lantern room with a resonance that seemed to shake the very walls. As she completed the incantation, a blinding flash of light erupted from the symbols on the floor, flooding the room with a searing, unearthly glow. The whispers reached a deafening crescendo, their voices merging into a single, anguished cry.

The light began to pulse and swirl, creating a vortex of energy that seemed to draw the shadows and whispers toward the centre of the room. The figurine of the lighthouse keeper glowed with an intense brightness, its form becoming almost translucent as it absorbed the energy of the ritual. The oppressive atmosphere that had plagued the lighthouse for so long seemed to be drawn into the vortex, the entity's presence growing weaker with each passing moment.

As the ritual reached its climax, the light and energy began to coalesce into a single, blinding burst. The shadows and whispers were pulled into the vortex, and Ella felt a surge of power that left her breathless. The light subsided, leaving the lantern room in a stunned silence. The oppressive atmosphere had lifted, and the room felt lighter and less menacing. The symbols on the floor had faded, their glow extinguished, and the shadows no longer writhed and twisted.

Ella's hands trembled as she surveyed the room. The entity's presence was gone, replaced by an eerie calm that settled over the lighthouse. The whispers had ceased, and the oppressive weight that had filled the space was now absent. The lantern room, though still old and weathered, felt more like a place of peace than a den of darkness.

As Ella collected her thoughts and documented her findings, she was filled with a mixture of relief and exhaustion. The ritual had been a success, but it had taken a toll on her both physically and emotionally. The artifact, now resting on the altar, was carefully examined and photographed. Ella's notes reflected her experience, detailing the changes in the lighthouse's atmosphere and the impact of the ritual on the entity.

The final moments of the ritual had left her with a profound sense of accomplishment. The lighthouse, though still an enigmatic structure, no longer harbored the malevolent presence that had plagued it. The ritual had lifted the darkness, but the experience had left a lasting impact on Ella. As she prepared to leave the lighthouse, she knew that her work was far from over. The mysteries of the lighthouse had been partially unveiled, but its history and secrets remained complex and multifaceted.

The storm that had once raged outside had passed, leaving the sea calm and the sky clear. The lighthouse stood against the twilight sky, a testament to the challenges Ella had faced and the victories she had achieved. As she drove away, she glanced back at the lighthouse, its silhouette now a symbol of her triumph over the darkness.

Her journey was far from over, and she knew that th lighthouse held more secrets yet to be discovered. The ritua had brought clarity and peace, but the echoes of the past anc the lingering mysteries would continue to shape her path. The lighthouse, with its dark history and enigmatic presence, had revealed its secrets, but the story was far from complete. As Ella continued her journey, she carried with her the knowledge that some mysteries are never fully resolved, but must be faced with courage and determination.

Chapter 10

The lighthouse stood silent against the backdrop of dawn, its formidable presence a stark contrast to the peaceful morning sky. Ella Parker's drive down the winding cliffside road was filled with a contemplative quiet. The ritual had been successful, yet she couldn't shake the feeling that her work was far from over. The lighthouse had been cleansed of its malevolent entity, but the deeper history and unresolved mysteries beckoned her to delve further.

Back in her temporary quarters at the nearby coastal inn, Ella spread out her notes and recordings on the small wooden table. The room, though cozy, felt stifling as if it held its own secrets. The artifacts and documents she had collected from the lighthouse were scattered around her. Her focus was on the leather-bound journal that had been central to the ritual. Its pages were filled with symbols and writings that hinted at a complex and dark past.

The journal had described a series of rituals and incantations that had been performed over the years. Each entry was dated and detailed, showing a gradual descent into madness and despair. The entries from the final days before the entity's first disappearance were particularly unsettling. They described a ritual that had gone awry, resulting in the entity's entrapment within the lighthouse. The descriptions were vague but hinted at a powerful and tragic event.

Ella's thoughts were interrupted by a knock on the door. It was the innkeeper, an elderly woman with a kind face and eyes that seemed to hold a lifetime of stories. She had brought a package for Ella, delivered by a local historian who had heard of her research. The package contained several old photographs and documents related to the lighthouse. Ella's curiosity piqued, she thanked the innkeeper and opened the package.

The photographs were of the lighthouse in various stages of its history. One photograph in particular caught her attention — a faded image of the lighthouse's first keeper, Edmund, standing proudly in front of the building. Beside him was Lydia, the woman mentioned in the letters Ella had found. Their faces were stern and resolute, but there was an undercurrent of sorrow in their expressions. The photograph was accompanied by a handwritten note that read: "For those who seek the truth, may you find the light."

Ella's heart raced as she examined the documents that accompanied the photographs. They were letters and personal accounts detailing the early years of the lighthouse. They spoke of strange occurrences and unexplained phenomena that predated the entity's arrival. The documents hinted at a deeper connection between the lighthouse and the local community, suggesting that the lighthouse was more than just a beacon for ships — it was a focal point for significant, yet undisclosed, events.

Determined to uncover more, Ella began cross-referencing the new documents with her existing research. The photographs and letters hinted at a secret society or a group of individuals who had a vested interest in the lighthouse's history. The more she delved into the documents, the clearer it became that the lighthouse had been the center of something much larger than a simple maritime legend.

One letter stood out among the rest. It was written in a shaky hand and addressed to someone named Jonathan. The letter described a secret meeting held by the society members, where they discussed the increasing disturbances at the lighthouse. The writer mentioned an ancient artifact hidden within the lighthouse that was believed to hold the key to controlling the entity. The letter was cryptic but suggested that this artifact had the power to either contain or release the dark force.

As she pored over the documents, Ella felt a growing sense of urgency. The lighthouse was not just a place of maritime history but a nexus of deeper, darker forces. The society's efforts to protect the lighthouse and its secrets revealed a profound legacy of guardianship and secrecy. The letters spoke of rituals and protective measures designed to keep the entity contained, but they also hinted at a growing fear that the entity might break free.

Ella decided to revisit the lighthouse, driven by a newfound sense of purpose. The documents suggested that there was still an artifact hidden within the lighthouse that could provide crucial insights into the entity and its connection to the lighthouse. The artifact's description matched some of the symbols and codes she had seen in the journal, and Ella felt that finding it might hold the key to understanding the full scope of the lighthouse's dark history.

Upon arriving back at the lighthouse, Ella felt a sense of renewed purpose. The building seemed to welcome her with a sense of calm that was in stark contrast to the oppressive atmosphere of before. The rituals had indeed cleansed the space, but the secrets that remained whispered of a legacy that was far from over.

She began her search by revisiting the areas she had previously explored. The hidden room with the nautical artifacts now felt different. The oppressive energy that had once filled the space was gone, replaced by a quiet stillness. She meticulously examined every item in the room, hoping to find something that might shed light on the connections hinted at by the new documents.

Her search led her to the old desk where she had previously found the letters from Lydia and Edmund. The desk's surface was now clean, revealing a hidden compartment she had missed before. Inside, she found more letters, some of which were written in a code that she had not yet deciphered. The letters spoke of meetings, codes, and a secret society dedicated to protecting the lighthouse and its secrets.

The letters provided a detailed account of the secret society known as "The Keepers of the Light." This group, it seemed, had been responsible for the lighthouse's maintenance and protection throughout its history. Their goal had been to guard the lighthouse's secrets and to prevent the entity from escaping or causing harm. The letters described rituals, codes, and protective measures that had been put in place to contain the darkness.

The coded messages were particularly intriguing. They hinted at a series of meetings and gatherings held in secret locations, where members of the society discussed the entity and its influence. Some letters contained cryptic instructions about rituals and protective wards that had been used to contain the entity. Others referenced historical events and figures connected to the lighthouse, providing a glimpse into a hidden network of individuals dedicated to preserving the balance between light and darkness.

Ella's heart raced as she pieced together the information. The lighthouse was not just a beacon for ships; it was a focal point for a much larger and darker narrative. The entity's presence was only one part of a greater story involving secret societies, hidden rituals, and a legacy of protection that spanned centuries.

Determined to uncover more, Ella continued her investigation. The more she learned, the more she realized that the lighthouse was a key element in a much larger narrative, one that involved not only the lighthouse keepers but also a hidden network of individuals dedicated to preserving their world from forces beyond comprehension. The artifacts, letters, and photographs were all pieces of a complex puzzle that was slowly coming together.

As the sun set over the lighthouse, she knew that the final chapters of its story were within reach. The journey had been arduous and filled with challenges, but the truth awaited her in the shadows. With the evidence she had gathered, she felt confident that she was on the cusp of uncovering the full extent of the lighthouse's dark history. The final pieces of the puzzle were falling into place, and Ella was ready to confront whatever lay ahead.

The night was still and quiet, save for the occasional creak of the old building. Ella's investigation was far from over, but she was one step closer to revealing the lighthouse's deepest secrets. As the darkness settled in, she prepared herself for the challenges and revelations that awaited her in the final chapters of the lighthouse's enigmatic story.

With each step of the ritual, the energy in the lantern room grew more intense. Ella moved the figurine in specific patterns, as instructed by the journal, channeling the ritual's energy through the intricate network of symbols. The room was filled with a growing, almost tangible force. The air crackled with static electricity, and the shadows on the walls seemed to stretch and contort in unnatural ways. The whispers, once mere background noise, were now a cacophony of voices, their tones rising and falling in a chaotic rhythm.

The ritual reached its apex with the final incantation, a powerful invocation intended to banish the entity and seal its influence. Ella recited the words with fervor, her voice echoing through the lantern room with a resonance that seemed to shake the very walls. As she completed the incantation, a blinding flash of light erupted from the symbols on the floor, flooding the room with a searing, unearthly glow. The whispers reached a deafening crescendo, their voices merging into a single, anguished cry.

The light began to pulse and swirl, creating a vortex of energy that seemed to draw the shadows and whispers toward the centre of the room. The figurine of the lighthouse keeper glowed with an intense brightness, its form becoming almost translucent as it absorbed the energy of the ritual. The oppressive atmosphere that had plagued the lighthouse for so long seemed to be drawn into the vortex, the entity's presence growing weaker with each passing moment.

As the ritual reached its climax, the light and energy began to coalesce into a single, blinding burst. The shadows and whispers were pulled into the vortex, and Ella felt a surge of power that left her breathless. The light subsided, leaving the lantern room in a stunned silence. The oppressive atmosphere had lifted, and the room felt lighter and less menacing. The symbols on the floor had faded, their glow extinguished, and the shadows no longer writhed and twisted.

Ella's hands trembled as she surveyed the room. The entity's presence was gone, replaced by an eerie calm that settled over the lighthouse. The whispers had ceased, and the oppressive weight that had filled the space was now absent. The lantern room, though still old and weathered, felt more like a place of peace than a den of darkness.

As Ella collected her thoughts and documented her findings, she was filled with a mixture of relief and exhaustion. The ritual had been a success, but it had taken a toll on her both physically and emotionally. The artifact, now resting on the altar, was carefully examined and photographed. Ella's notes reflected her experience, detailing the changes in the lighthouse's atmosphere and the impact of the ritual on the entity.

The final moments of the ritual had left her with a profound sense of accomplishment. The lighthouse, though still an enigmatic structure, no longer harbored the malevolent presence that had plagued it. The ritual had lifted the darkness, but the experience had left a lasting impact on Ella. As she prepared to leave the lighthouse, she knew that her work was far from over. The mysteries of the lighthouse had been partially unveiled, but its history and secrets remained complex and multifaceted.

The storm that had once raged outside had passed, leaving the sea calm and the sky clear. The lighthouse stood against the twilight sky, a testament to the challenges Ella had faced and the victories she had achieved. As she drove away, she glanced back at the lighthouse, its silhouette now a symbol of her triumph over the darkness.

Her journey was far from over, and she knew that the lighthouse held more secrets yet to be discovered. The ritual had brought clarity and peace, but the echoes of the past and the lingering mysteries would continue to shape her path. The lighthouse, with its dark history and enigmatic presence, had revealed its secrets, but the story was far from complete. As Ella continued her journey, she carried with her the knowledge that some mysteries are never fully resolved, but must be faced with courage and determination.

Chapter 10

The lighthouse stood silent against the backdrop of dawn, its formidable presence a stark contrast to the peaceful morning sky. Ella Parker's drive down the winding cliffside road was filled with a contemplative quiet. The ritual had been successful, yet she couldn't shake the feeling that her work was far from over. The lighthouse had been cleansed of its malevolent entity, but the deeper history and unresolved mysteries beckoned her to delve further.

Back in her temporary quarters at the nearby coastal inn, Ella spread out her notes and recordings on the small wooden table. The room, though cozy, felt stifling as if it held its own secrets. The artifacts and documents she had collected from the lighthouse were scattered around her. Her focus was on the leather-bound journal that had been central to the ritual. Its pages were filled with symbols and writings that hinted at a complex and dark past.

The journal had described a series of rituals and incantations that had been performed over the years. Each entry was dated and detailed, showing a gradual descent into madness and despair. The entries from the final days before the entity's first disappearance were particularly unsettling. They described a ritual that had gone awry, resulting in the entity's entrapment within the lighthouse. The descriptions were vague but hinted at a powerful and tragic event.

Ella's thoughts were interrupted by a knock on the door. It was the innkeeper, an elderly woman with a kind face and eyes that seemed to hold a lifetime of stories. She had brought a package for Ella, delivered by a local historian who had heard of her research. The package contained several old photographs and documents related to the lighthouse. Ella's curiosity piqued, she thanked the innkeeper and opened the package.

The photographs were of the lighthouse in various stages of its history. One photograph in particular caught her attention — a faded image of the lighthouse's first keeper, Edmund, standing proudly in front of the building. Beside him was Lydia, the woman mentioned in the letters Ella had found. Their faces were stern and resolute, but there was an undercurrent of sorrow in their expressions. The photograph was accompanied by a handwritten note that read: "For those who seek the truth, may you find the light."

Ella's heart raced as she examined the documents that accompanied the photographs. They were letters and personal accounts detailing the early years of the lighthouse. They spoke of strange occurrences and unexplained phenomena that predated the entity's arrival. The documents hinted at a deeper connection between the lighthouse and the local community, suggesting that the lighthouse was more than just a beacon for ships — it was a focal point for significant, yet undisclosed, events.

Determined to uncover more, Ella began cross-referencing the new documents with her existing research. The photographs and letters hinted at a secret society or a group of individuals who had a vested interest in the lighthouse's history. The more she delved into the documents, the clearer it became that the lighthouse had been the center of something much larger than a simple maritime legend.

One letter stood out among the rest. It was written in a shaky hand and addressed to someone named Jonathan. The letter described a secret meeting held by the society members, where they discussed the increasing disturbances at the lighthouse. The writer mentioned an ancient artifact hidden within the lighthouse that was believed to hold the key to controlling the entity. The letter was cryptic but suggested that this artifact had the power to either contain or release the dark force.

As she pored over the documents, Ella felt a growing sense of urgency. The lighthouse was not just a place of maritime history but a nexus of deeper, darker forces. The society's efforts to protect the lighthouse and its secrets revealed a profound legacy of guardianship and secrecy. The letters spoke of rituals and protective measures designed to keep the entity contained, but they also hinted at a growing fear that the entity might break free.

Ella decided to revisit the lighthouse, driven by a newfound sense of purpose. The documents suggested that there was still an artifact hidden within the lighthouse that could provide crucial insights into the entity and its connection to the lighthouse. The artifact's description matched some of the symbols and codes she had seen in the journal, and Ella felt that finding it might hold the key to understanding the full scope of the lighthouse's dark history.

Upon arriving back at the lighthouse, Ella felt a sense of renewed purpose. The building seemed to welcome her with a sense of calm that was in stark contrast to the oppressive atmosphere of before. The rituals had indeed cleansed the space, but the secrets that remained whispered of a legacy that was far from over.

She began her search by revisiting the areas she had previously explored. The hidden room with the nautical artifacts now felt different. The oppressive energy that had once filled the space was gone, replaced by a quiet stillness. She meticulously examined every item in the room, hoping to find something that might shed light on the connections hinted at by the new documents.

Her search led her to the old desk where she had previously found the letters from Lydia and Edmund. The desk's surface was now clean, revealing a hidden compartment she had missed before. Inside, she found more letters, some of which were written in a code that she had not yet deciphered. The letters spoke of meetings, codes, and a secret society dedicated to protecting the lighthouse and its secrets.

The letters provided a detailed account of the secret society known as "The Keepers of the Light." This group, it seemed, had been responsible for the lighthouse's maintenance and protection throughout its history. Their goal had been to guard the lighthouse's secrets and to prevent the entity from escaping or causing harm. The letters described rituals, codes, and protective measures that had been put in place to contain the darkness.

The coded messages were particularly intriguing. They hinted at a series of meetings and gatherings held in secret locations, where members of the society discussed the entity and its influence. Some letters contained cryptic instructions about rituals and protective wards that had been used to contain the entity. Others referenced historical events and figures connected to the lighthouse, providing a glimpse into a hidden network of individuals dedicated to preserving the balance between light and darkness.

Ella's heart raced as she pieced together the information. The lighthouse was not just a beacon for ships; it was a focal point for a much larger and darker narrative. The entity's presence was only one part of a greater story involving secret societies, hidden rituals, and a legacy of protection that spanned centuries.

Determined to uncover more, Ella continued her investigation. The more she learned, the more she realized that the lighthouse was a key element in a much larger narrative, one that involved not only the lighthouse keepers but also a hidden network of individuals dedicated to preserving their world from forces beyond comprehension. The artifacts, letters, and photographs were all pieces of a complex puzzle that was slowly coming together.

As the sun set over the lighthouse, she knew that the final chapters of its story were within reach. The journey had been arduous and filled with challenges, but the truth awaited her in the shadows. With the evidence she had gathered, she felt confident that she was on the cusp of uncovering the full extent of the lighthouse's dark history. The final pieces of the puzzle were falling into place, and Ella was ready to confront whatever lay ahead.

The night was still and quiet, save for the occasional creak of the old building. Ella's investigation was far from over, but she was one step closer to revealing the lighthouse's deepest secrets. As the darkness settled in, she prepared herself for the challenges and revelations that awaited her in the final chapters of the lighthouse's enigmatic story.

Chapter 11

Ella Parker moved with a determined sense of purpose as the early morning light cast long, pale shadows across the lighthouse. The storm had finally abated, leaving behind an eerie calm. The lighthouse, though quieter now, held a palpable tension, as if holding its breath in anticipation of what was to come. The time had come for Ella to confront the Shadow of the Abyss and unlock the final mysteries that had haunted this forsaken place.

The previous night had been a whirlwind of preparation. Ella had meticulously gathered all her findings — the letters detailing the lighthouse keeper's fears, the ancient journal describing the ritual, the strange artifacts, and the eerie symbols. Each piece had led her to this moment, where her actions would determine the fate of the lighthouse and perhaps something far greater.

In the dim light of dawn, she methodically set up her equipment in the central chamber of the lighthouse, the room she believed to be the focal point for the final ritual. The ancient symbols etched into the walls seemed to pulse with an ominous energy, as if they were aware of the impending confrontation. She arranged the ritual components with precision: the tarnished compass, the ornate box with intricate carvings, and the carved figurine of the lighthouse keeper. Each item had been examined thoroughly, and Ella had deciphered their connections to the ritual described in the ancient journal.

The ritual began with Ella drawing the symbols on the floor in chalk, their intricate designs glowing faintly as she worked. The air grew colder, charged with an otherworldly energy that made her breath visible in the dim light. As she placed the various components in their designated positions and began chanting the ancient incantations, the atmosphere around her seemed to grow heavier.

The lighthouse itself seemed to react to her actions. The old beams groaned and trembled as if the building were alive and aware of the ritual's progress. Shadows on the walls twisted and writhed in unnatural ways, converging on the central chamber. A low, guttural growl filled the air, reverberating through the structure. The first true manifestation of the Shadow of the Abyss appeared — a swirling vortex of darkness that defied natural laws. It was a grotesque, amorphous mass of malevolent energy, with tendrils of shadow reaching out like grasping hands. The entity's form was ever-shifting, a pulsating blackness that seemed to absorb all light around it.

Ella's heart raced as she faced the dark entity. Her hands trembled, but she forced herself to continue the ritual. The symbols on the floor began to glow with an ethereal light, pushing back against the encroaching darkness. The air crackled with energy as the entity's form distorted and flickered, struggling against the ritual's power. The dissonant chorus of whispers, growls, and screams filled the room, trying to shatter her concentration. The voices clawed at her sanity, echoing her deepest fears and insecurities.

Despite the chaos, she pressed on. She realized that the entity's power was tied to the fear and despair it had instilled in the lighthouse's previous inhabitants. The shadows and whispers were not merely distractions — they were manifestations of the entity's power, feeding off the fears it had cultivated over the years. To weaken the entity, she needed to confront not only the dark force but also her own inner demons. With renewed determination, she channeled her personal struggles into the ritual, integrating her own fears and triumphs into the ancient incantations. This revelation was crucial; her inner strength and resolve helped to diminish the entity's influence.

The ritual reached its peak as she invoked the final incantations. The room was bathed in blinding light, the symbols glowing fiercely as they fought against the darkness. The entity writhed and shrieked, its form breaking apart under the strain of the ritual. The vortex of shadows began to collapse in on itself, the tendrils retreating and the growls fading into distant, echoing wails. Ella's voice rose above the din, her words a beacon of hope and defiance. The lighthouse seemed to resonate with her will, its ancient structure coming alive with a force that pushed the entity back into its prison.

The final incantation sealed the breach, and the light from the symbols flared brightly, closing the rift and imprisoning the Shadow of the Abyss once more. The oppressive atmosphere lifted, replaced by a heavy silence that spoke of peace restored. The lighthouse, once again, felt like a guardian of the sea rather than a prison of darkness. The shadows on the walls receded, leaving behind a sense of calm that was both soothing and surreal.

Ella collapsed to the floor, exhausted but triumphant. Her breath came in ragged gasps as she took in the transformed space around her. The air was lighter, and the temperature had returned to a more bearable level. The lighthouse, though still ancient and weathered, no longer carried the oppressive weight of malevolence that had hung over it. The strange symbols and artifacts that had played such a crucial role in the confrontation were now mere remnants of a dark chapter in the lighthouse's history.

Ella took a moment to collect her thoughts. The Shadow of the Abyss was a dark entity, a remnant of ancient fears and malign energies, but it had been contained. The lighthouse was no longer a gateway to darkness but a beacon of light and history. The letters, journal, and artifacts had all contributed to this victory, and she felt a deep sense of accomplishment.

Her thoughts turned to the future. The lighthouse would need repairs, and its history needed to be preserved. There were still many questions to answer and many details to uncover, but for now, Ella had succeeded in her primary goal. The darkness had been driven back, and the lighthouse's secrets had been unveiled.

As she prepared to leave, she took one last look around the lighthouse. The light of dawn streamed through the broken panes, casting a gentle glow over the restored space. The lighthouse stood as a testament to the enduring strength of those who had faced its darkness and prevailed. Ella felt a sense of closure and renewal, knowing that she had played a crucial role in preserving its legacy.

With a final glance at the ancient symbols and the artifacts that had been crucial to the confrontation, she stepped outside into the crisp morning air. The lighthouse, once a place of dread and mystery, now stood as a symbol of resilience and hope. For Ella, the journey had been one of discovery and courage, and as she made her way back to civilization, she knew that the lighthouse would remain a beacon of both history and light.

Chapter 12

The lighthouse stood silent and still as dawn's first light cast a serene glow over the rugged coastline. The storm had passed, leaving behind a cleansed landscape — a sharp contrast to the tumultuous night that had just ended. Ella Parker gazed at the lighthouse with a sense of deep relief and accomplishment, her heart swelling with a mixture of pride and exhaustion.

The air was crisp and invigorating, carrying the fresh scent of saltwater and the promise of a new beginning. The lighthouse, bathed in the golden hues of morning, looked less like a relic of fear and more like a steadfast sentinel that had weathered the worst of nature's wrath. Ella could see the intricate details of its structure more clearly now, the faded paint and rust that had once seemed so menacing now blending harmoniously with the light.

She had spent a long, gruelling night performing the ritual to seal away the Shadow of the Abyss. The entity that had haunted the lighthouse for so long was now confined, its influence diminished. The air inside the lighthouse felt lighter, as if a great burden had been lifted. The walls, once shrouded in an oppressive darkness, now seemed to breathe with a newfound vitality.

As Ella walked towards the lighthouse, she felt a profound connection to the place. It had been a constant presence in her life over the past weeks, its mysteries and challenges shaping her in ways she had not anticipated. She paused to take in the surroundings — the overgrown vegetation, the remnants of the storm, and the stillness that now reigned supreme. It was as though the lighthouse had finally found its peace, and in turn, so had Ella.

Her immediate task was to ensure that all her findings were properly documented. She meticulously packed her equipment, checking and rechecking to make sure that nothing was left behind. The artifacts she had discovered, including the old maps, the cryptic journal, and the strange symbols, were crucial pieces of history. She knew that her work was far from over; these artifacts needed to be preserved and studied to ensure that the lighthouse's story would be told accurately and respectfully.

As she gathered her things, Ella's thoughts turned to Dr. Margaret Caldwell, the local historian who had been a supportive ally throughout her investigation. Margaret had expressed a keen interest in assisting with the final documentation and restoration. Ella knew that Margaret's expertise would be invaluable in ensuring that the lighthouse's story was shared with a wider audience. She made a mental note to contact Margaret once she returned to civilization.

Before leaving, she took one last, lingering look at the lighthouse. The ritual symbols etched into the floor, now faded but still discernible, were a testament to the struggle that had taken place. Ella traced the symbols with her gaze, remembering the intense moments of the night — the rituals, the confrontations, and the eerie manifestations. The lighthouse, with all its secrets and dangers, had become an integral part of her journey, and she felt a deep sense of closure.

Her departure from the lighthouse was both a physical and emotional journey. As she drove away, the landscape gradually shifted from the rugged coastline to rolling hills and open fields. The serenity of the countryside contrasted sharply with the turmoil she had faced in the lighthouse. The road ahead was open, symbolizing new opportunities and adventures.

Her thoughts were filled with reflections on her experiences. The investigation had been a harrowing ordeal, but it had also been an opportunity for personal growth and discovery. Ella had faced her fears, confronted the darkness, and emerged with a greater understanding of both the lighthouse and herself. The entity that had haunted the lighthouse, once a source of terror, had been vanquished, and she had played a crucial role in that triumph.

As she drove, she thought about the broader implications of her findings. The lighthouse had not only been a site of supernatural activity but also a focal point for historical research. The letters, journal, and artifacts she had uncovered would provide valuable insights into the past, shedding light on the lives of those who had come before her. She hoped that her work would contribute to a greater understanding of the lighthouse's history and the challenges it had faced.

The sun climbed higher in the sky, casting a warm, reassuring light over the landscape. Ella felt a sense of renewal and optimism. The lighthouse, once a symbol of darkness and fear, had been transformed into a beacon of hope and resilience. Its story would be preserved, and its legacy would be honored.

Ella's journey was far from over. The world was full of stories waiting to be uncovered, and she was eager to embrace the next chapter of her life. Her experiences at the lighthouse had strengthened her resolve and deepened her appreciation for the mysteries of history. She knew that there would be new challenges and discoveries ahead, and she welcomed them with anticipation.

As she approached the edge of the town, she saw the familiar landmarks that marked the return to civilization. The transition from the lighthouse's isolation to the bustling activity of the town was both jarring and comforting. She felt a sense of accomplishment and readiness for the next phase of her journey.

In the days that followed, Ella worked closely with Dr. Caldwell and other local historians to document and preserve the lighthouse's story. The artifacts were carefully cataloged, and the findings were shared with the community. The lighthouse, once a place of fear and darkness, had become a symbol of human perseverance and the triumph of light over shadow.

Ella's work was recognized and celebrated, and she felt a deep sense of satisfaction knowing that her efforts had made a difference. The lighthouse's story was now a part of the broader narrative of maritime history, and its legacy would continue to inspire and inform future generations.

As she prepared to leave the town and embark on her next adventure, she took one final look at the lighthouse. It stood proudly against the horizon, its silhouette a poignant reminder of the challenges it had faced and the victories it had achieved. Ella knew that the lighthouse would always hold a special place in her heart, and its story would be a part of her own.

With a renewed sense of purpose, she set out on the road, ready to embrace whatever lay ahead. The lighthouse had been a profound chapter in her life, but it was time to move forward. The world was full of new horizons and untold stories, and Ella was eager to explore them.

As she drove into the distance, the lighthouse faded from view, but its impact remained. The journey had been transformative, and Ella felt ready to face the future with courage and determination. The lighthouse's legacy of light and hope would continue to guide her, wherever her path might lead.

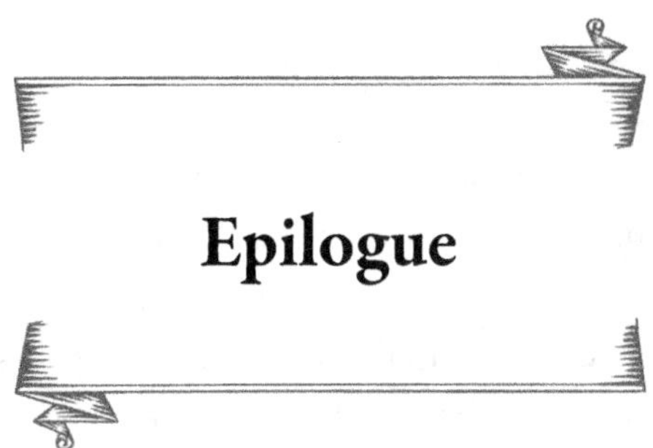

Epilogue

Years had passed since Ella Parker had left the old lighthouse behind. The lighthouse had been lovingly restored, its weathered exterior now a proud testament to its storied past. It stood as a beacon not only for ships but for those who came seeking the tales and mysteries of the past. The once-dilapidated structure had been transformed into a vibrant historical site, its corridors and rooms now filled with artifacts and exhibits that told the story of its tumultuous history and the brave souls who had guarded it.

Ella had become a celebrated historian, her work on the lighthouse earning her acclaim and respect in the field of maritime history. Her detailed research and documentation had brought the lighthouse's story to life for countless visitors. The old logbooks, letters, and artifacts were now displayed in a dedicated museum section, allowing people to glimpse the shadows and secrets that had once haunted its walls.

Despite the passage of time, Ella remained deeply connected to the lighthouse. She often visited, finding solace in its restored beauty and the knowledge that its history was being honored and preserved. The eerie presence that had once loomed over the structure was now a part of the past, but the lighthouse's stories continued to captivate and intrigue.

On one such visit, Ella was approached by a young historian named Claire Thompson, who had recently joined the team working at the lighthouse museum. Claire had come across an old journal that Ella had never seen before — a journal that hinted at another layer of mystery surrounding the lighthouse. The entries spoke of a hidden chamber and cryptic symbols that suggested there were still untold stories waiting to be discovered.

Ella felt a familiar thrill of excitement as she read through Claire's findings. The sense of adventure and curiosity that had driven her through the trials of her investigation was rekindled. As she gazed out at the lighthouse, its silhouette against the setting sun, she knew that while her own journey had reached a satisfying conclusion, the lighthouse's story was far from over.

With renewed purpose, Ella decided to assist Claire in unravelling the new mystery. The lighthouse had always been a place of secrets, and now, it seemed that another chapter was about to unfold. The shadows that had once haunted the lighthouse were now a part of its legacy, and the promise of new discoveries beckoned.

As Ella and Claire prepared to delve into the new mysteries, the lighthouse stood as a symbol of perseverance and discovery. Its light continued to shine, guiding not only ships but those who sought to uncover the truths hidden within its walls. The journey was far from over, and for Ella, it was a reminder that the pursuit of knowledge and the quest for understanding were endless.

The old lighthouse, with its rich history and enduring mysteries, had found a new chapter, and Ella Parker was ready to embrace it. The adventure continued, and the lighthouse's legacy

of light and hope would forever guide those who dared to seek
its secrets.

75

About the Author

David J Cooper is a writer who spends more time in the company of ghosts and paranormal legends than in the everyday world. His novels dive deep into the world of paranormal mysteries and spectral secrets. When not researching haunted places or crafting chilling tales, David can be found walking his dogs. He calls Brixham home, where he continues to explore the unknown with a pen in hand and a curious spirit.